The Big
Red Trouble

CARMEN HARRIS

About this book

When Richard first sees the
Scarletron XR2 car in the junk shop
window he knows he has to have it.
It's second-hand and not quite perfect
but it still costs a lot. Wherever will
he get so much money?
Somehow Richard finds the money
and buys the car. He doesn't have
much fun with it. It turns out to be
The Big Red Trouble!

About the author

Carmen Harris was born in Jamaica,
and has lived in Britain since she was
five. She has worked in community
theatre and as a journalist, and writes
for stage and television. She lives in
London with her teenage daughter.

A BANANA BOOK

The Big Red Trouble

CARMEN HARRIS

Illustrated by
PATRICIA LUDLOW

HEINEMANN · LONDON

For the children of
Lancasterian Junior School

William Heinemann Ltd
Michelin House
81 Fulham Road
London SW3 6RB

LONDON   MELBOURNE   AUCKLAND

First published in 1991
Text © Carmen Harris 1991
Illustrations © Patricia Ludlow 1991
ISBN 0 434 97679 2

Printed in Italy
by Olivotto

A school pack of BANANA BOOKS 43–48 is
available from Heinemann Educational Books
ISBN 0 435 00107 8

Chapter One

RICHARD HAD A two week holiday and nothing to do. He headed for Mr Trembly's sweet shop counting pigeon-steps. Trust Akim to go off to Manchester to stay with his cousins! Akim was his best friend who lived six doors away.

Richard stopped at every shop on the way and looked in all the windows, counting up to a hundred before moving on. First the chip shop, then the launderette, then the greengrocers, then

1

the shoe menders. By the time he reached the secondhand shop he had counted a hundred at every shop window and done four hundred and thirteen pigeon steps between them. Normally he'd walk straight past this shop. There was never anything worth looking at through the dirty windows. But this time something caught Richard's eye. In the middle of the pile of junk was a cardboard box and on top of it was a red car. But it wasn't just *any* red car. Richard couldn't believe his eyes. He pressed his face against the window and gaped at all the knobs and buttons and levers and lights. Through the dusty pane he could just make out the writing on the side of the box: 'Scarletron XR2 . . . Action Parts . . . Four-wheel Independent Super Suspension . . . Lifesaver Ejector Seat . . . Eight Speed Gear Box . . .

Laser Jet Headlights . . .
Demon Driver . . .
Instruction Booklet.
Bargain. Only £4.50.'

How he would love to own that car!

When he got to Mr Trembly's
sweetshop he'd lost all his interest in

3

sweets. He handed over his fifteen pence and walked out with a bag of chews he didn't even want.

On the way home he had to pass the secondhand shop again. The shiny headlights of the car looked like two big eyes staring at him. They seemed to be saying, 'I'm *only* £4.50.'

'Sorry,' said Richard glumly, 'if I had £4.50 I'd be inside buying you right now.'

Chapter Two

RICHARD'S FATHER WORKED nights, so now he was fast asleep in the downstairs bedroom. Richard tiptoed inside to put the key back in the pocket of his father's jacket. His hand brushed against something. It was his father's wallet. A daring thought suddenly popped into Richard's head. What if he *borrowed* £4.50 from his dad? The thought stayed in Richard's head and his hand stayed on the wallet. He gently lifted it out of the pocket and slipped quietly into the kitchen.

When he spread all the notes on the table his eyes widened with amazement. His father couldn't possibly miss a measly

£4.50. *And* it was going to be paid back! He separated a five pound note and replaced the rest of the money in the wallet. In a few seconds he was out in the street again.

As he pushed open the door of the musty shop a bell tinkled and a shaky voice called out in the dark.

'Yes son?'

'Can I have that car? The car in the window,' Richard said breathlessly.

'It costs £4.50, you know,' the man behind the counter said.

'I have it here,' said Richard, holding out the crushed five pound note.

'You'd better look at it first,' advised the old man, 'It's not new and I can't guarantee it'll do all it's supposed to do. I don't want you coming here tomorrow asking for your money back.'

He picked up the car and handed it to Richard. The old man was right, it wasn't new – but then Richard already knew that. He tried the lever for the ejector seat. It flipped upwards on the end of a spring. That seemed to work all right.

'Does the laser jet work?' he asked.

'Don't ask me, son,' said the old man. 'What you see is what you get.'

'Okay, I'll have it,' Richard said.

The shopkeeper shrugged his shoulders, 'Just as long as you know you've been warned,' he said, taking the £5 note and handing back fifty pence.

Richard turned the car over and over as he walked towards the door.

'Haven't you forgotten something?' called the old man, pointing to the box on the floor. 'You'll want something to keep it in, won't you?'

Chapter Three

WITH AN ENORMOUS smile on his face, Richard walked down the road carrying the box with the car safely packed inside. Two boys passing by stared at him and shouted, 'Cor, look at that, a Scarletron XR2!'

Richard's smile grew even bigger. But it wasn't long before it disappeared. The moment he reached his front door he realised what he had done. He had taken money from his father's pocket! He had *stolen* money! He was nothing but a *thief*! Suddenly he wasn't excited any more. He was scared.

Richard crept through the front door. He peeped into the downstairs bedroom. His father was still asleep. With his heart thumping against his chest Richard

tiptoed towards the chair to put the
change in his father's wallet.

'GGGGG ZZZZZ GGGGG ZZZZZ!'
Richard dropped the wallet and ran. It
was only while he was trembling outside
the door that he realised what the noise
was. His father's snoring! *Now* what was
he going to do? Perhaps he should wait till
Mum got home and own up about what
he'd done. He rushed upstairs and put the
car in his wardrobe, but his clothes were
hanging too high to cover it. He tried his

toy box but that was full up. Then he
remembered the cupboard under the
stairs where all the junk was kept. He'd
put it there. No one ever went in there.

At a quarter past four when he heard

his mother's key turn in the lock, Richard
rushed to meet her.

'Hello Ricky. What a day I've had!' she
sighed. 'I haven't stopped since this
morning. Did you eat your lunch? Hope

11

you didn't wake your father. What are
those empty sweet wrappers doing on the
floor? I hope you haven't spoilt your
appetite for dinner. We're having
liver . . . don't make a face, it's good for
you . . . '

'Mum . . . ' Richard began.

'Not now, Ricky – later,' she called,
rushing upstairs to the loo. Richard's
heart sank. He knew by the time she came
down again he would have lost his courage.

Chapter Four

RICHARD'S FATHER WAS downstairs getting out of bed and his mother was frying liver in the kitchen.

'Ricky, dinner,' she called.

The thought of liver, and the thought of being found out made his stomach do a sickly somersault.

'Mum, I'm not feeling well,' he groaned from the top of the stairs.

'Come on, I know your tricks,' said his mother, peering up the stairs. But when she saw how pale Richard looked she said, 'Okay. You'd better get into bed.'

Richard jumped straight into his pyjamas and into bed. His white face matched his pillow and he was shivering. He could hear his mother and father arguing . . . about money!

'Mary, have you taken money from my pocket?'

'What are you talking about?'

'Money's missing from my wallet.'

'You're a fine one! You already owe me for the milk.'

'Well, did you?'

'I did no such thing!'

This was too much for Richard. He pulled the blanket over his head and tried to blot it all out. Then he heard his father's footsteps coming up the stairs.

'Richard?' said the deep voice at his bedside.

Richard held his breath under the blanket and pretended he was under water and if he breathed he would drown.

'Richard?' said his father again.

Richard wasn't much good at swimming, but he'd rather drown than face his dad.

'Richard . . . '

His father seemed to stand over him for ages. As soon as Richard heard him turn away, he let out a long sigh of relief. By the time his father's footsteps reached the kitchen Richard could hear him saying, 'He's asleep, Mary. You're right. There must be something wrong with him . . . I must have lost that note.'

'Well don't forget you still owe me the milk money,' said Mum.

Chapter Five

WHENEVER HIS MOTHER or father walked past the hall cupboard Richard's heart flipped up to his throat. Imagine! He had the world's greatest car, but he was too frightened even to peep at it.

Saturday came at last and Akim would be back in two days' time. Richard sat at the kitchen table crushing toast crumbs with his fingernails while his mother put the laundry into the washing machine.

'All week,' she was saying, 'all week you've been playing with your food and moping around the house. You'll have to go and see Dr Rawlinson if I don't see an improvement soon. Now, I'm spring cleaning today. It's about time I moved that old chest out of your room. I'll ask your father to help me put it in the cupboard under the stairs.'

THE CUPBOARD UNDER THE STAIRS!

Richard's chair tumbled to the ground, carrying him with it.

He looked up at his mother.

'Richard! What's got into you? Get up off the floor you clumsy thing.'

'Mum!' shouted Richard, 'there's someone upstairs!'

'It's probably your dad. Fancy him coming in and not saying. You clear away the plates. I'll go and have a look.'

As soon as his mother began to climb the stairs, Richard threw open the cupboard door and pulled out the box. He had to get it out of sight, and fast! The car felt quite heavy as he ran through the rain towards the old shed. Was the car growing bigger or did he imagine it?

When he got back inside his mother was
just coming down the stairs.

'Richard! What *have* you been up to?'
she shouted.

Richard stood in the middle of the
kitchen dripping from head to toe. A pool
of water slowly collected on the lino
around his squelching slippers.

'I-I've been out for a walk.'

'A *walk*? In the rain! Have you gone
mad? Get up those stairs and dry yourself
off before you catch a cold!'

Chapter Six

LATER THAT DAY Richard and his mum
and dad sat at the table having dinner.
Richard pushed his untouched plate to
one side and when the doorbell rang he
was glad for the excuse to leave the table.
But then his mother said,

'That'll be the old man from the
secondhand shop come to collect
the chest of drawers.'

Richard suddenly froze
half-on, half-off his seat.

'Well go on, love, answer
the door,' said
his mother.

'I can't,' he said.

'What do you mean,
you can't?' asked
his father.

'I have to go,' replied Richard, rushing upstairs and locking himself in the toilet.

'What did I tell you? There's something wrong with that boy,' said his mother. 'You'd better take him to see Dr Rawlinson on Monday.'

Chapter Seven

ON SUNDAY RICHARD'S mother and father sat in the living room reading the papers. Richard stood in the hallway trying to figure out when to sneak the car back into the house. Now was the time, he decided. Then he heard his mother sigh,

'Oh well, time to start the lunch I suppose.'

Richard froze outside the door.

Next he heard his father shake out the paper and say,

'I'll see what's wrong with that mower and do a bit of weeding.'

Richard was already heading for the back door. He'd have to be double quick!

The box was on its side behind a bag of compost where he had thrown it. When he picked up the heavy box he almost

dropped it. He lifted the lid and saw the car
was bursting out of the box. He tried to
think of where to hide it next. There was
only one place – the dustbin.

He dashed across the garden and
unlatched the gate to the side of the
house. On Saturday his mother had put a
pile of rubbish beside the bins. He
dumped the box on top.

'Richard?' said his father's voice,
'What are you doing out there?'

'N-Nothing.'

'Is this yours?'

Richard's heart missed a beat.

His father held a white ticket in his hand.
It read 'Bargain. Only £4.50.'

'N-No, Dad.'

His father turned the cardboard over in
his hands and looked at it with a frown.
Then he shrugged his shoulders and
pushed it towards Richard.

'Put it in the bin. It must have blown
over from next door,' he said.

Chapter Eight

THE WHIRRING, CLANKING and banging of the rubbish truck woke Richard the next morning. He leapt out of bed, remembering that the car was still beside the dustbins. Jumping down five steps at a time he landed barefoot at the front door. He carefully turned the catch and stood at the doorway looking out.

'Hello, son. What are you doing up so early?'

A man wearing a woolly hat and a ragged pair of gloves opened the gate and disappeared down the side of the house. He came back with a dustbin slung over one shoulder and a black plastic bag in his hand.

'I left my car . . . ' Richard whispered.

'Hang on, son,' he shouted, 'is this it?'

Richard's face fell when he saw the soggy cardboard box.

'Where's the car?' he asked.

'Is this what you're looking for?' grinned the man, producing the Scarletron from the bin.

Richard blinked and gasped, 'Th-Thanks.'

He couldn't believe the size of the car. It had grown so big, he would *never* be able to hide it. Suddenly he didn't want the car any more.

BEEEEP! BEEEEP! BEEEEP!

Richard almost dropped the car at the sound of his mother's alarm clock. He heard his mother getting out of bed.

'Ricky,' she called.

The cupboard under the stairs was the nearest place to hide. Richard opened the door and disappeared inside.

'Ouch!'

Something hard stubbed his toe and he hopped about on one leg in the dark. But when he heard his mother call again he

stood as still as a statue. Would she look in
his room and find that he wasn't in bed?
Why was his life so difficult? Anyone
would think he was James Bond!

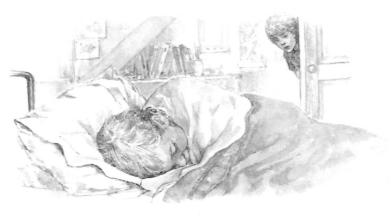

Five minutes later his mother walked
past his room and peeped in. She saw the
lump in the bed and decided that all was
well. Richard smiled to himself beneath
the blankets and wondered if James Bond
could have done better with a nearly
broken toe.

Chapter Nine

AKIM WAS BACK.

'Look at this Rick!' he yelled, whizzing down the road on his new skateboard.

'Can I have a go?' Richard shouted.

'Not yet!' called Akim.

'Oh come on! You've had four goes,' Richard complained.

But Akim was now trying to do some fancy footwork.

'Okay – I won't let you have a go with my new car,' sulked Richard.

Akim stopped. 'What car?' he asked.

'A Scarletron XR2,' Richard boasted.

'Never heard of it,' said Akim.

'Well you should have. It's got a laser jet that shoots real lasers,' said Richard, forgetting to add that not all the parts were working.

'Okay,' said Akim, 'let's do a swop.'

'We'll have to get it first.'

'Come on then,' said Akim.

'Be quiet, though. My father's asleep,' warned Richard.

They tiptoed into the house and quietly made their way up to Richard's bedroom. Richard opened the bottom drawer of his chest and pulled out a pile of underwear. At the bottom lay the Scarletron XR2.

When Akim's mouth fell open, so did Richard's.

The big red thing had grown even more, and Richard was now scared of it.

'It's m . . . mega, isn't it?' he said uncertainly.

'It's wicked, man!' said Akim, 'but why's it under all your clothes?'

'Er, um, in case we get burgled,' mumbled Richard.

Akim held the car above his head. Richard followed with the skateboard and off they went to the top of the hill.

'On your marks . . . Go!' shouted Akim, and they raced to the bottom, Richard on the skateboard and Akim speeding behind with the Scarletron XR2.

'In the name of the Space Police, this is your last warning – stop now! Okay, that's it, Skate Creature! Get ready for a blast of XR2!'

Akim didn't seem to care that the laser jet wasn't working, or that there weren't

any batteries to make the car go. They
were both having a lot of fun. When
Akim's older brother came out to tell him
that it was time to go in, they were both
very disappointed.

Richard was happy for the first time in a
week. Smiling, he cradled the car under
his arm and pushed open his front door.
But the smile suddenly disappeared. His
father was standing in the hall.

Chapter Ten

'WHERE'VE YOU BEEN Richard? And what's that you've got?'

'I-It's a car,' Richard stuttered.

'Yes, I can see that,' said his father, 'but whose is it?'

'I-It's . . . um, I borrowed it,' he said.

'Well take it back. We're going to the doctor's.'

'Yes, Dad.'

Richard closed the door and turned to face the street. What was he going to do *now*? If he asked Akim to look after it, he'd have to tell him the truth – that he'd stolen money to buy the car. He sat on the step and put the car in front of him. Suddenly he hated the big red trouble. It kept reminding him of what he'd done and all the lies he'd told. And the more lies he told the bigger the car seemed to grow. There was only one thing to do.

He got up and walked up the road with the car under his arm. The door of the shop tinkled as he pushed it open.

'Yes, son?'

'Please, can I have my money back. I don't want this any more,' said Richard.

'You're the boy who came in last week,' said the old man, 'this isn't a library you know. You don't borrow things and bring them back when you've had your fun.'

'But I haven't had any fun,' Richard cried, 'except for today, and even then my friend, Akim, played with the car instead of me.'

'And why was that?' asked the old man.

Richard looked down at his shoes.

'Because . . . ' he began, but he couldn't go on.

'Cars don't grow for no reason at all,' said the old man.

Richard looked up. 'Cars don't grow at all!' he was about to say. But the way the old man was staring at him over his glasses made him blurt out, 'I stole the money to buy it.'

The old man shook his head slowly and made a disapproving noise under his breath. It was a long time before he reached into the pocket of his holey cardigan and said,

'I can only give you £3.50.'

'But I need £4.50,' Richard said desperately. 'Here's the fifty pence change. I need a five pound note.'

The old man looked at the coin in Richard's hand. 'You should have thought of that before,' he said.

Chapter Eleven

RICHARD SAT ON his bed folding and unfolding the crisp five pound note. At last he had all the money – but at a price. He had to promise the old man that he'd come back and clean his dirty windows.

He heard the front door open and his mother come in. He screwed up the note and put it into his pocket.

'Ricky!'

'Yes, Mum.'

'Did you go to Dr Rawlinson?'

'Yes, Mum.'

'What did he say?'

'I'm okay.'

'Well, you could have fooled me.'

'Mum, can I go down the road for half an hour?'

'What for?'

'I've got a job.'

'A job? What kind of job?'

'Cleaning windows. I promised the man at the secondhand shop.'

'Cleaning windows? Have you seen the state of your room lately?'

'Aw please, Mum.'

'Oh, all right. But don't be late for dinner,' she shouted back.

As he went down the stairs he noticed his mother's bag, hanging on the bannister. Quickly he pulled out her purse and slipped in the five pound note.

'Here's your milk money, Mum.'

A smile spread across his face. Mission Accomplished.

When he opened the door there was another smiling face on the doorstep.

'Rick, can you come out for half an hour?' cried Akim excitedly.

'I'm going somewhere,' Richard replied.

'Where are you going?'

'Never you mind.'

'All right. I won't tell you about my surprise,' said Akim jumping and leaping around excitedly.

'Okay. I'll listen if you help me wash someone's windows.'

'Yeah!' Akim agreed. 'Guess, then!'

'I can't guess. Just get on with it.'

'No, you've got to guess!'

'Someone's bought you something.'

'Right! Go on, guess some more.'

'New clothes?' growled Richard.

'No, it's a car! I've got a car!' Akim
shouted.

Richard slowed down.

'My dad bought it for me! It's a
Scarletron XR2, just like yours.'

Richard stopped dead.

'What's wrong?' Akim asked.

Suddenly Richard let out a whoop of
joy. He grabbed Akim's skateboard and
sped down the street. He was free! He had
got rid of the car. He had paid the stolen
money back. He would never steal again.
And now Akim had a Scarletron XR2 –
they could both take turns with it!

Akim raced after him. 'Hey, wait for
me!' he shouted.

A BANANA BOOK